Copyright © 1993 by Nord-Süd Verlag AG, Gossau Zürich, Switzerland
First published in Switzerland under the title *Rotkäppchen*
English translation copyright © 1993 by North-South Books Inc.

First published in the United States, Great Britain, Canada,
Australia, and New Zealand in 1993 by North-South Books,
an imprint of Nord-Süd Verlag AG, Gossau Zürich, Switzerland.

Distributed in the United States by North-South Books Inc., New York.

Library of Congress Cataloging in Publication Data
Grimm, Jacob, 1785-1863.
[Rotkäppchen]
Little Red Cap : a fairy tale / translated from the German
by Anthea Bell ; with pictures by Monika Laimgruber.
Summary: A little girl meets a hungry wolf in the forest
while on her way to visit her grandmother.
ISBN 1-55858-167-7 (trade binding)
ISBN 1-55858-168-5 (library binding)
[1. Fairy tales. 2. Folklore—Germany.] I. Grimm, Wilhelm, 1786-1859.
II. Bell, Anthea. III. Laimgruber, Monika, ill. IV. Title.
PZ8.G882Lj 1993
398.2—dc20
[E] 93-19923

British Library Cataloguing in Publication Data
Grimm, Jacob
Little Red Cap
I. Title II. Grimm, Wilhelm
III. Bell, Anthea IV. Laimgruber, Monika
823.914
ISBN 1-55858-167-7

1 3 5 7 9 10 8 6 4 2
Printed in Belgium

Little Red Cap

A fairy tale by Jacob and Wilhelm Grimm
Translated from the German by Anthea Bell
With pictures by Monika Laimgruber

NORTH-SOUTH BOOKS • NEW YORK

Once upon a time there was a sweet little girl. Everyone who knew her loved her. Her grandmother loved her most of all, and she never tired of giving the child presents. One day she gave her a cap made of red velvet. It was very becoming, and the little girl liked it so much that she wore it all the time, so she was known as Little Red Cap.

One day her mother said, "Now, Little Red Cap, here's some cake and a bottle of wine. I want you to take them to Grandmother. She's feeling poorly, and they will do her good. You must set off before it gets hot, and mind you're a good girl! Don't stray from the path, or you might fall and break the bottle, and then there'd be nothing left for Grandmother. And when you get to Grandmother's house, remember to say good morning, and don't go looking all around the house first."

"I'll do just as you say," Little Red Cap promised her mother.

Grandmother lived quite a long way off in the forest, half an hour's walk from the village. As Little Red Cap went into the forest, she met a wolf, but since she didn't know what a wicked creature he was, she wasn't afraid of him.

"Good morning, Little Red Cap," said the wolf.

"Thank you kindly, wolf."

"And where are you going so early, Little Red Cap?"

"I'm going to see my grandmother."

"What's that in your basket?"

"Cake and wine. I'm taking them to poor sick Grandmother to do her good."

"Where does your grandmother live, Little Red Cap?"

"Oh, another quarter of an hour's walk into the forest. Her house stands under the three big oak trees, with the hazelnut hedges in front of it," said Little Red Cap. "I'm sure you know the place."

The wolf was thinking, "This tender young thing will make a nice meal! She'll taste even better than the old lady. But if I go about it cunningly, I can catch them both."

So he walked on with Little Red Cap for a while, and then he said, "See those pretty flowers growing everywhere, Little Red Cap! Why don't you look around you? Do you hear how sweetly the little birds sing? You're just walking straight ahead as if you were hurrying to school, and it's such fun out here in the forest."

Little Red Cap looked around, and when she saw the sunbeams dancing through the trees, and all the beautiful flowers, she thought, "Grandmother would be pleased if I brought her a bunch of flowers, and it's so early that I'm sure to get to her house in good time." So she left the path and went into the forest looking for flowers. Whenever she picked a flower, she saw a prettier one growing a little farther on and ran to pick that one too. Soon she had strayed deeper and deeper into the forest.

The wolf hurried off to Grandmother's house and knocked on the door.

"Who is it?"

"Little Red Cap, with some cakes and wine for you. Open the door!"

"Just lift the latch," called Grandmother. "I'm feeling too poorly to get up."

So the wolf lifted the latch, opened the door, and without so much as a word went straight over to Grandmother's bed and gobbled her up. Then he put on one of her nightgowns and a nightcap, got into her bed, and drew the curtains.

All this time Little Red Cap had been picking flowers, and when she had such a big bunch that she could hardly carry it, she remembered Grandmother and set off for her house. She was surprised to find the door already open, and when she went in, there seemed to be something very strange about the house. "Oh dear," she thought. "This place makes me feel so scared today. I usually love coming to Grandmother's!"

"Good morning," she called, but there was no reply. So she went over to the bed and pulled back the curtains. There lay Grandmother in her nightcap, looking very odd.

"Oh, Grandmother, what big ears you have!"
"All the better to hear you with, my dear."
"Oh, Grandmother, what big eyes you have!"
"All the better to see you with, my dear."
"Oh, Grandmother, what big hands you have!"
"All the better to hug you with, my dear."
"And oh, Grandmother, what big teeth you have!"
"All the better to eat you with, my dear!" And no sooner had the
wolf said that than he jumped out of bed and gobbled up poor Little
Red Cap.

Now that the wolf had eaten his fill, he went back to bed, and
soon was snoring very loudly.

A huntsman happened to be walking past the house just then. "Listen to the old lady snoring!" he thought. "I'd better go and see if there's anything wrong with her."

So he went into the house and walked over to the bed, where he saw the wolf fast asleep. "So here you are, you old sinner!" said the huntsman. "I've been after you for a long time." And he was about to aim his gun when it struck him that the wolf might have swallowed Grandmother whole. Perhaps he could still save her, so he didn't fire the gun. Instead, he took a pair of scissors and began cutting open the sleeping wolf's stomach. As soon as he had snipped a few times, he saw the bright red of the little girl's cap. Another couple of snips, and out jumped Little Red Cap herself, crying, "Oh, how scared I was! It was so dark inside the wolf!"

Then Grandmother too came out of the wolf safe and sound, although she could scarcely breathe. Little Red Cap found some big stones and put them into the wolf's stomach. When he woke up, he tried to run away, but the stones were so heavy that he tumbled to the floor and fell down dead.

All three of them felt very pleased. The huntsman skinned the wolf and took the skin home. Grandmother ate the cake that Little Red Cap had brought and soon was feeling better. As for Little Red Cap, she said to herself, "As long as I live, I'll never again stray from the path and go into the forest when Mother tells me not to."